GRACIE La Roo

AT TRAINING CAMP

written by **MARSHA QUALEY**

illustrated by **KRISTYNA LITTEN**

raintree

a Capstone company — publishers for children

Raintree is an imprint of Capstone Global Library Limited, a company
incorporated in England and Wales having its registered office at 264
Banbury Road, Oxford, OX2 7DY – Registered company number: 6695582

www.raintree.co.uk
myorders@raintree.co.uk

Designed by Hilary Wacholz
Original illustrations © Capstone Global Library Limited 2019
Originated by Capstone Global Library Ltd
Printed and bound in India

ISBN 978 1 4747 7012 5
22 21 20 19 18
10 9 8 7 6 5 4 3 2 1

British Library Cataloguing in Publication Data
A full catalogue record for this book is available from the British Library.

CONTENTS

GRACIE and The

NAME: Gracie LaRoo

TEAM: Water Sprites

CLAIM TO FAME:
Being the youngest pig
to join a world-renowned
synchronized swimming team!

SIGNATURE MOVE:
"When Pigs Fly" Spin

LIKES: Purple, clip-on tail bows,
mud baths, newly mown hay
smell

DISLIKES: Too much attention,
doing laundry, scary films

QUOTE

"I just hope I can be the kind of synchronized
swimmer my team needs!"

Water Sprites

JINI

BARB

JIA

SU

MARTHA

BRADY

SILVIA

TOGETHER AGAIN

Gracie LaRoo looked around the table in the busy dining hall. She smiled as the other Water Sprites talked about their holidays.

The team was back together for training camp. A new swimming season was just around the corner!

"Why are you smiling, Gracie?" Jini asked. Jini was the team captain.

"Because it's wonderful to be together again. My holiday was nice, but I missed you all so much. I've been looking forward to being here," Gracie said, yawning.

The yawn grew wider and wider until it collapsed into a soft squeal.

"Gracie has made a good
point," Jini said. "It is very late.
We should all go to bed. Tomorrow
we will start training for the new
season. We will need energy."

Silvia said, "We are scheduled to take our turn in the pool first thing in the morning."

Several Sprites started talking at the same time.

"Not in the morning!" said Jia.

"I need to finish some music for our new opening routine," said Barb.

"I haven't finished the new swimming costume design," added Brady.

"We have to finish the new poster!" Su and Martha said.

Jini sighed. "I suppose I can swap times with the water basketball team."

While the others cheered Jini's decision, Gracie said nothing. She wanted to be in the pool with the team as soon as possible.

This is not how she thought training camp would start.

CHAPTER 2

GRACIE ALONE

The next morning, Gracie ate breakfast by herself. Other tables were filled with teams that were laughing and talking.

Gracie scraped off her dirty plate into the bin alongside a baseball team.

She exercised in the fitness room while an athletics team lifted weights.

She got in the lift with a
basketball team.

When Gracie stepped out of
the lift, she didn't hear a thing.
The corridor was quiet. Where
were her teammates?

Just then, Brady stuck her head out of her room.

"Gracie!" she said. "Come here."

Brady's room was a mess! There were drawings and pieces of fabric everywhere.

"I've been making new swimming costumes, but I can't work out what's wrong. Try this on," Brady said.

Gracie shimmied into the costume. She raised her hooves, wiggled and then spun around.

"It doesn't quite fit. The shoulders are a little tight," Gracie said.

"That's it! Thanks, Gracie!" Brady said.

She turned to her drawing pad and began sketching again.

Gracie changed back into her clothes and left. Barb poked her head out of her room.

"Gracie!" she said. "Come here."

Barb had a piano keyboard in her room. She sat and played a short tune.

"Wouldn't that be great for a new routine?" Barb asked.

"It's a wonderful melody," Gracie said, "but the tempo is a little fast."

"That's it! Thanks, Gracie!" Barb said.

She tapped a few keys, humming along.

Gracie slipped out of the room. So far training camp didn't include much training.

THE FIGHT

Martha and Su were at the end of the corridor. Gracie was happy to see more of her teammates.

"Pool practice has been moved to this evening," said Su.

"Why?" Gracie asked. "We need to be together."

"We asked Jini to change it again because everyone is so busy," said Martha.

Martha and Su went into a room and closed the door.

Gracie was frustrated. When would they swim? She stamped a hoof.

Today certainly didn't feel like a team sort of day. In her room, she changed into a swimming costume.

Gracie tried to practise by herself, pretending she was in a pool.

She stamped her hoof again. She needed water to practise!

She needed her team.

Gracie sat on her bed and tried to read. Soon, she heard doors opening and closing. She heard voices outside her room.

"Jini, there you are!" That was Brady.

"Jini, I have an idea!" That was Barb.

"Look at the new poster!" Martha and Su said together.

They were talking about costumes and schedules and music and posters. Soon everyone was arguing about what was most important and what should be done first.

Gracie opened her door.

"Why are you all fighting?" she shouted. "Why aren't we in the pool? We are a swimming team. We should be swimming together, not fighting! That's what's important."

No one said a word as Gracie

stamped her hoof, slammed her

door and marched to the lift –

alone.

CHAPTER
4

THAT'S OUR GRACIE

The pool was empty. Gracie sat

on the edge of the pool and kicked

the water. The

splashing echoed

loudly. She rose

and walked to the

diving board.

She bounced. She bounced

higher. She bounced higher still.

She pushed off on
the next bounce and
started spinning.

Once around.

Twice around.

Three times around.

Then she was
sliding into the water.
Gracie dropped to
the bottom and sat.

She blew bubbles until she needed more air.

When Gracie returned to the surface, a wave of cheers greeted her. Jini's voice was the loudest.

"What a perfect triple spin!" she called.

"That's our Gracie!" shouted Silvia.

Now all the Sprites were in the water with Gracie.

Barb said, "You were right, Gracie."

"We're a water ballet team," Brady said.

"We do our best in the water. Other things can wait," said Jia.

The team jumped, splashed and swam for hours.

Gracie smiled as she looked at the lights and water and colours around her. She was only a little bit dizzy.

Oh, how she loved swimming. Oh, how she loved her team!

GLOSSARY

collapsed suddenly fell away

design make a pattern or drawing

frustrated feeling annoyed

melody main part of a song that is usually repeated

routine sequence of moves in a dance or synchronized swimming performance

shimmied wriggled

sketch rough drawing

tempo how fast or slow a song is being played

TALK ABOUT IT!

1. Do you think it would be hard to be the captain of a team? Why?

2. Talk about a time when you weren't happy with your friends.

3. Do you think Gracie was being a good friend? Why or why not?

WRITE ABOUT IT!

1. Write about a training camp you would like to attend.

2. Pretend you are Gracie and make a daily training schedule for the team.

3. What would it be like to be one of Gracie's teammates? Write a story from that point of view.

Marsha Qualey is the author of many books for readers young and old. Though she learned to swim when she was very young, she says she has never tried any of the moves and spins Gracie does so well.

Marsha has four grown-up children and two grandchildren. She lives in Wisconsin, USA, with her husband and their two non-swimming cats.

About the illustrator

Kristyna Litten is an award winning children's book illustrator and author. After studying illustration at Edinburgh College of Art, she now lives and works in Yorkshire with her pet rabbit, Herschel.

Kristyna would not consider herself a very good swimmer as she can only do the breaststroke, but when she was younger, she would do a tumble roll and a handstand in the shallow end of the pool.

THE WONDERFUL, THE AMAZING, THE PIG-TASTIC GRACIE LAROO!

Discover more at
www.raintree.co.uk